GRAPHIC NATURAL DISASTERS
VOLCANOES

by Rob Shone
illustrated by Terry Riley

rosen
central™
The Rosen Publishing Group, Inc., New York

Published in 2007 by The Rosen Publishing Group, Inc.
29 East 21st Street, New York, NY 10010

Copyright © 2007 David West Books

First edition, 2007

Designed and produced by
David West Books

Editor: Gail Bushnell

Photo credits:
p6bl, Lancevortex; p6br, USGS; p6tr Richard P. Hoblitt, USGS; p7tr, USGS Photograph taken on May 18, 1980, by Austin Post; p44tr, NASA; p44m, USGS; p45t, USGS Photograph taken on September 24, 1981, by Thomas J. Casadevall; p45bl, NASA; p45br, USGS Photograph taken in August 1984, by Lyn Topinka.

Library of Congress Cataloging-in-Publication Data

Shone, Rob.
  Volcanoes / by Rob Shone ; illustrated by Terry Riley.
    p. cm. -- (Graphic natural disasters)
  Includes index.
  ISBN-13: 978-1-4042-1988-5 (library binding)
  ISBN-10: 1-4042-1988-9 (library binding)
  ISBN-13: 978-1-4042-1976-2 (6 pack)
  ISBN-10: 1-4042-1976-5 (6 pack)
  ISBN-13: 978-1-4042-1975-5 (pbk.)
  ISBN-10: 1-4042-1975-7 (pbk.)
  1. Volcanoes--Juvenile literature. I. Title.
  QE521.3.S5375 2007
  551.21--dc22

                                    2006032882

Manufactured in China

CONTENTS

WHAT IS A VOLCANO?   4

KILLER VOLCANOES   6

VESUVIUS, A.D. 79   8

KRAKATOA, 1883   18

MOUNT ST. HELENS, 1980   28

STUDYING VOLCANOES   44

GLOSSARY   46

FOR MORE INFORMATION   47

INDEX and WEB SITES   48

WHAT IS A VOLCANO?

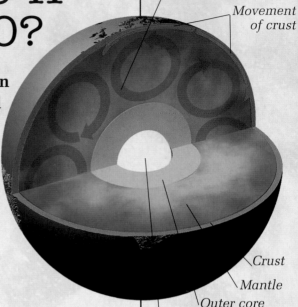

Rotating currents

Movement of crust

From under the Earth's thin crust, molten rock, called magma, forces its way to the surface. When it reaches the surface it is called lava and it flows like molasses. As each successive layer of lava cools, a mountain gradually develops into a volcano.

A PLANET OF LAYERS

At the center of the Earth is an inner, and outer, core. Around this is the mantle, an area of hot, slowly moving rock. Rotating currents within this layer cause sections, or plates, of the thin outer crust to move in different directions. It is at the boundaries of these plates that most volcanoes appear.

Crust

Mantle

Outer core

Inner core

A cutaway of the Earth (above) shows the layers in a simplified form. The map below shows the distribution of the world's volcanoes.

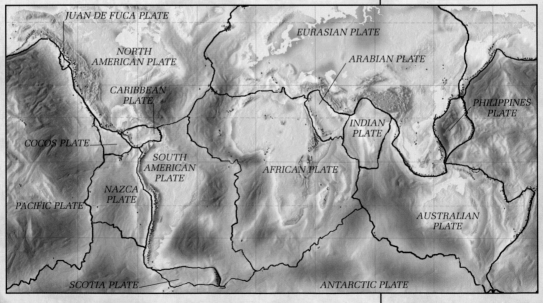

JUAN DE FUCA PLATE

EURASIAN PLATE

NORTH AMERICAN PLATE

ARABIAN PLATE

CARIBBEAN PLATE

PHILIPPINES PLATE

COCOS PLATE

INDIAN PLATE

SOUTH AMERICAN PLATE

AFRICAN PLATE

NAZCA PLATE

PACIFIC PLATE

AUSTRALIAN PLATE

SCOTIA PLATE

ANTARCTIC PLATE

• Volcano   ——   Plate boundaries

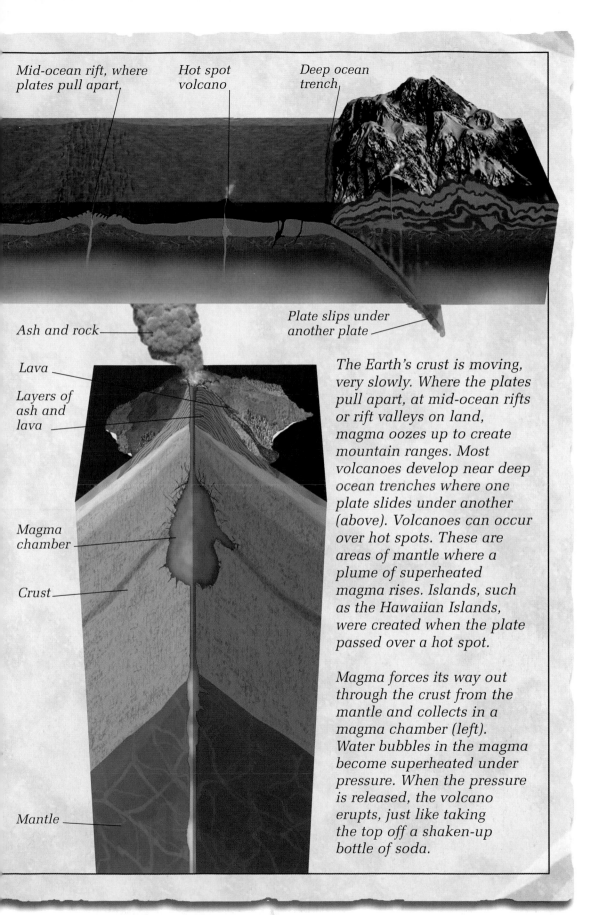

Mid-ocean rift, where plates pull apart

Hot spot volcano

Deep ocean trench

Plate slips under another plate

Ash and rock

Lava

Layers of ash and lava

Magma chamber

Crust

Mantle

The Earth's crust is moving, very slowly. Where the plates pull apart, at mid-ocean rifts or rift valleys on land, magma oozes up to create mountain ranges. Most volcanoes develop near deep ocean trenches where one plate slides under another (above). Volcanoes can occur over hot spots. These are areas of mantle where a plume of superheated magma rises. Islands, such as the Hawaiian Islands, were created when the plate passed over a hot spot.

Magma forces its way out through the crust from the mantle and collects in a magma chamber (left). Water bubbles in the magma become superheated under pressure. When the pressure is released, the volcano erupts, just like taking the top off a shaken-up bottle of soda.

KILLER VOLCANOES

The violence of an eruption depends on the amount of silica and water in the rising magma. The silica determines how runny the rock is. The water provides the explosive force of pressurized steam.

EXPLOSIONS

If the eruption is violent enough, whole volcanoes can disappear. Santorini, in Greece, and Krakatoa, in Indonesia, both blew tens of cubic miles (cubic kilometers) of rock and ash into the atmosphere. Volcanic islands such as these produce large waves called tsunamis, which can devastate coastal areas for thousands of miles (or kilometers). When the magma is less runny, volcanoes can spit out lumps of lava, called bombs, over a mile (two kilometers) away.

2. Ash and rock mixed with rain or snow form rivers of flowing sludge, called lahars. In the Philippines, Sapangbato (above) was one of many villages destroyed by lahars from the erupting Pinatubo in 1991.

3. Hot ash clouds, between 392 °F (200 °C) and 1,292 °F (700 °C), speed down the Mayon in the Philippines (below). Known as pyroclastic flows, these clouds travel over 150 mph (241 km/h) and burn anything in their path.

1. Hot ash and rock form a tall column, called a plinian column. Collapsing columns can bury whole cities in ash, suffocating the inhabitants within minutes, as with Pompeii (left).

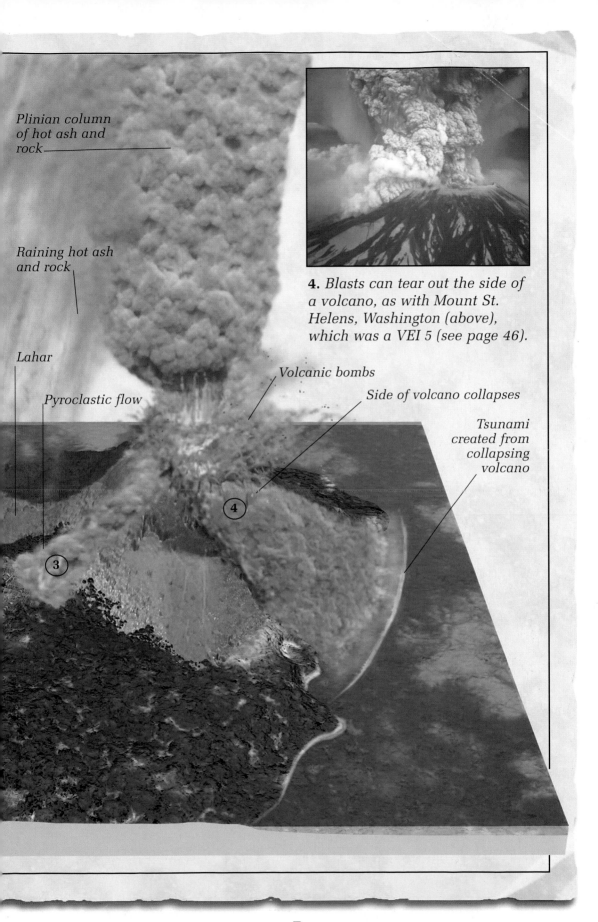

Plinian column of hot ash and rock

Raining hot ash and rock

Lahar

Pyroclastic flow

Volcanic bombs

Side of volcano collapses

Tsunami created from collapsing volcano

4. Blasts can tear out the side of a volcano, as with Mount St. Helens, Washington (above), which was a VEI 5 (see page 46).

③

④

VESUVIUS, A.D. 79

POMPEII, AUGUST 24, 1:00 P.M. JULIUS POLYBIUS WAS AT HOME WITH HIS WIFE.

JULIUS, HOW MUCH LONGER WILL ALL THIS BUILDING WORK LAST? THE DUST GETS EVERYWHERE.

IF I AM ELECTED AN AEDILE* WE WILL BE ENTERTAINING IMPORTANT PEOPLE. THE HOUSE MUST LOOK ITS BEST.

*A ROMAN OFFICIAL

AND THAT'S ANOTHER THING, THE EXPENSE. DON'T AEDILES HAVE TO PAY FOR SOME PUBLIC WORKS THEMSELVES?

DON'T WORRY, MY BAKERIES ARE MAKING US ENOUGH MONEY.

AND I'LL MAKE SURE THE BUILDERS FINISH THE WORK AS QUICKLY AS POSSIBLE.

9

...FOLLOWED BY A ROAR AS MOUNT VESUVIUS EXPLODED.

KARRRDOOOM!!

I'VE NEVER SEEN A MOUNTAIN DO **THAT** BEFORE!

A HUGE BLACK CLOUD DRIFTED TOWARD POMPEII.

SUDDENLY...

...THE SKY RAINED PUMICE STONES.

THE STREETS FILLED WITH PEOPLE TRYING TO ESCAPE.

I DON'T THINK JULIUS POLYBIUS WILL WANT THE WORK FINISHED TODAY.

NOT EVERYONE HAD LEFT THE CITY.

JULIUS, THE SERVANTS HAVE LEFT. SHOULDN'T WE GO TOO?

WE MUST STAY CALM. THIS WILL NOT LAST LONG, I AM SURE. WE WILL BE SAFE HERE.

THAT EVENING THE VOLCANO STARTED TO LOSE ITS STRENGTH.

THE HUGE FIERY COLUMN OF ASH COLLAPSED...

...AND SENT A PYROCLASTIC FLOW TOWARD POMPEII'S NEIGHBORING TOWN, HERCULANEUM.

NEARLY EVERYONE HAD LEFT HERCULANEUM. A FEW PEOPLE REMAINED.

THEY WERE ALL KILLED AS THE TOWN WAS BURIED UNDER 60 FEET (18 METERS) OF BURNING RUBBLE.

THE FLOWS HAD NOT REACHED POMPEII YET. PEOPLE WERE STILL TRYING TO ESCAPE.

THE WEIGHT OF THE PUMICE CAUSED ROOFS TO COLLAPSE ON THOSE THAT STAYED.

KEERRAKK!!

AT THE HOUSE OF JULIUS POLYBIUS...

MY LOVELY GARDEN IS RUINED. WE SHOULD HAVE GONE WHEN WE HAD THE CHANCE.

WE WOULD NOT HAVE GOTTEN FAR AT OUR AGE. BESIDES, WHEN THIS IS ALL OVER AND POMPEII IS BACK TO NORMAL, THE PEOPLE WILL NEED A GOOD BAKER.

AT 6:00 A.M., A SURGE OF HOT POISONOUS GAS SWAMPED POMPEII.

JULIUS POLYBIUS AND HIS WIFE WAITED FOR THE END TO COME.

NONE SURVIVED.

16

LIKE HERCULANEUM THE NOW-LIFELESS CITY WAS BURIED.

AFTER 19 HOURS THE ERUPTIONS STOPPED.

POMPEII AND HERCULANEUM WERE ABANDONED, AND IN TIME FORGOTTEN. THEY WERE REDISCOVERED IN 1599 BY AN ARCHITECT NAMED FONTANA. IT WAS NOT UNTIL THE MID-1700'S THAT WORK STARTED TO UNEARTH THEM. TODAY THEY ARE BOTH IMPORTANT ARCHAEOLOGICAL SITES. MOUNT VESUVIUS LAST ERUPTED IN 1944. SCIENTISTS BELIEVE ANOTHER ERUPTION IS DUE.

THE END

KRAKATOA, 1883

IT WAS MONDAY, AUGUST 27, AND THE STEAMSHIP LOUDON HAD JUST SURVIVED ITS THIRD TSUNAMI OF THE MORNING.

THE SHIP WAS ANCHORED IN LAMPONG BAY OUTSIDE THE TOWN OF TELOK BELONG, SUMATRA. ON BOARD WERE 111 PASSENGERS AND CREW.

IT HAD BEEN AN EFFORT FOR THE CAPTAIN, JOHAN LINDEMAN, TO STOP THE SHIP FROM CAPSIZING.

40 MILES (64 KILOMETERS) SOUTH OF THE LOUDON LAY THE VOLCANIC ISLAND OF KRAKATOA. THE DAY BEFORE, AT 1:00 P.M., IT HAD COME TO LIFE, SENDING ASH AND PUMICE INTO THE AIR.

ON MONDAY MORNING THE ISLAND EXPLODED THREE TIMES AND THEN FELL SILENT. THE CAUSE OF THE ERUPTIONS LAY DEEP BENEATH THE THREE CRATERS. MILLIONS OF TONS OF MOLTEN ROCK HAD BEEN HURLED OUT OF ITS MAGMA CHAMBER.

NOW THE CHAMBER WAS ALMOST EMPTY.

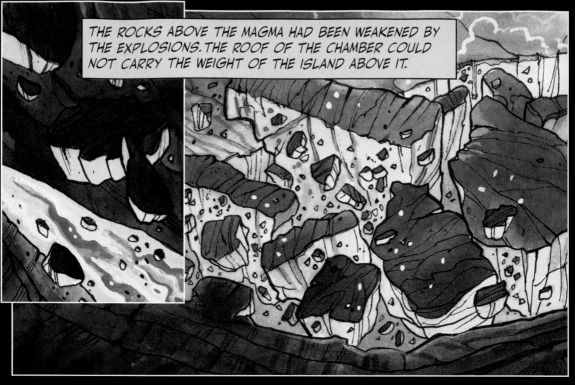

THE ROCKS ABOVE THE MAGMA HAD BEEN WEAKENED BY THE EXPLOSIONS. THE ROOF OF THE CHAMBER COULD NOT CARRY THE WEIGHT OF THE ISLAND ABOVE IT.

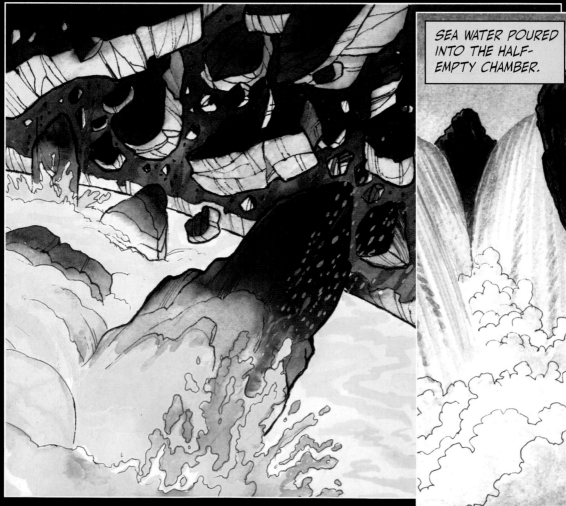

SEA WATER POURED INTO THE HALF-EMPTY CHAMBER.

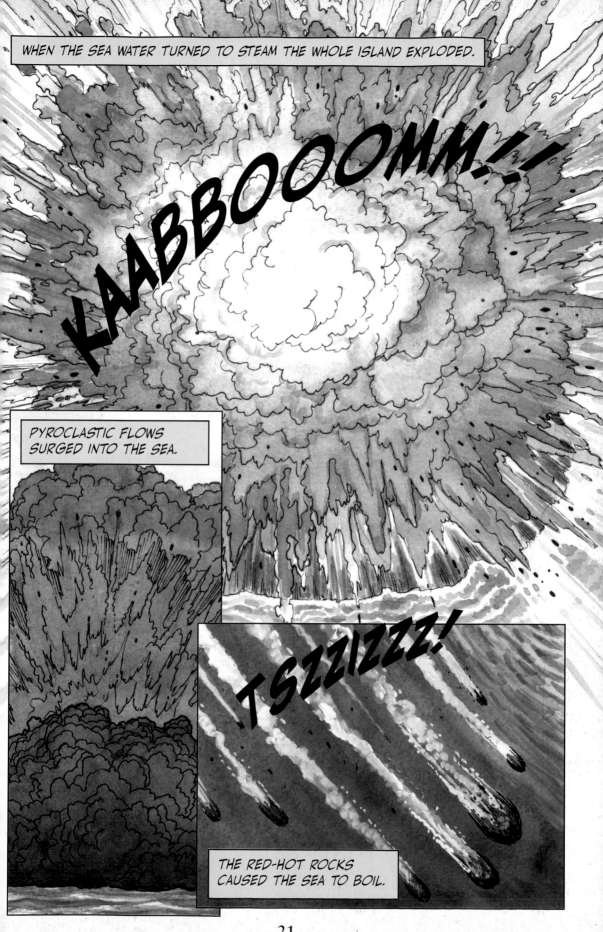

WHEN THE SEA WATER TURNED TO STEAM THE WHOLE ISLAND EXPLODED.

KAABBOOOMM!!!

PYROCLASTIC FLOWS SURGED INTO THE SEA.

TSZZIZZZ!

THE RED-HOT ROCKS CAUSED THE SEA TO BOIL.

THE EXPLOSION TRIGGERED A MASSIVE TSUNAMI.

BAARRISSHH...

THE LOUDON MANAGED TO SAIL OVER IT.

THE WAVE MOVED TOWARD THE LAND.

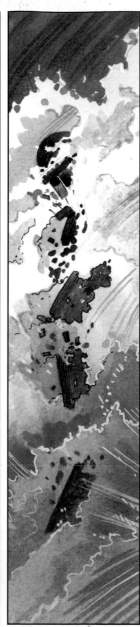

AT TELOK BELONG...

23

THE WAVE SMASHED INTO THE HARBOR...

BDOOOSHH!!!

...AND CARRIED ON INLAND.

AT SEA THE LOUDON WAS ROCKED BY HURRICANE-FORCE WINDS.

PASSENGERS AND CREW WORKED TO CLEAR THE DECK OF THICK MUD RAIN. SOME BECAME ILL DUE TO THE VOLCANO'S TOXIC FUMES.

MEANWHILE, A PYROCLASTIC FLOW, RIDING ON A BED OF STEAM, HAD TRAVELED 25 MILES (40 KILOMETERS) TO THE COAST OF SUMATRA.

BY TUESDAY MORNING THE ERUPTION WAS OVER. THE LOUDON SAILED FOR JAVA.

PUMICE STONE, 20 FEET (6 METERS) DEEP, COVERED THE SEA.

THE PUMICE HAD CREATED WHOLE NEW ISLANDS.

NEARLY EVERY LIGHTHOUSE HAD BEEN WRECKED.

THEY SAW A DEVASTATED COASTLINE EVERYWHERE THEY PASSED.

THE STEAMSHIP BEROUW WAS FOUND NEARLY A MILE (ONE AND A HALF KILOMETERS) INLAND FROM TELOK BELONG HARBOR.

ALL THAT WAS LEFT OF KRAKATOA WAS A CLIFF FACE.

IN 1967 THE CRATER WHERE KRAKATOA HAD BEEN CAME TO LIFE. OVER THE NEXT FEW YEARS A NEW ISLAND GREW AND IS STILL GROWING. IT WAS NAMED ANAK KRAKATOA, WHICH MEANS CHILD OF KRAKATOA.

THE END

MOUNT ST. HELENS, 1980

SATURDAY, MAY 17, 1980. HARRY TRUMAN HAD VISITORS AT HIS SPIRIT LAKE LODGE.

FOR THE LAST TIME, I'M STAYING RIGHT HERE!

I'VE LIVED NEXT TO THAT MOUNTAIN FOR 50 YEARS AND I'M NOT LEAVING NOW!

OKAY, OKAY, HARRY. WE WERE JUST PASSING AND THOUGHT WE WOULD STOP BY.

THE SCIENTISTS AT VANCOUVER THINK IT COULD ERUPT AT ANY TIME.

SCIENTISTS! WHAT DO THEY KNOW! SURE, IT BLOWS OFF A LITTLE STEAM AND ASH EVERY NOW AND THEN – BUT THAT DOESN'T MEAN ANYTHING.

WELL, YOU'RE THE LAST ONE HERE, HARRY. EVERYONE ELSE HAS GONE. IF YOU CHANGE YOUR MIND LET US KNOW.

I WON'T BE CHANGING MY MIND.

NORTH OF MOUNT ST. HELENS, ON THE GREEN RIVER, MIKE AND LU MOORE HAD SET UP CAMP WITH THEIR TWO DAUGHTERS, BONNIE LU AND TERRE.

BONNIE LU! YOU COME AWAY FROM THERE THIS MINUTE.

IT'S ONLY AN OLD HUNTING SHACK.

IT LOOKS LIKE IT COULD FALL DOWN ANY SECOND, AND THIS PLACE IS DANGEROUS ENOUGH.

MIKE, ARE YOU SURE WE'RE GOING TO BE SAFE HERE? ST. HELENS ISN'T THAT FAR AWAY.

LU, WE'RE NEARLY 15 MILES FROM THE MOUNTAIN. THERE ARE THREE TALL RIDGES AND THREE DEEP VALLEYS BETWEEN US AND IT.

WHATEVER COMES OUT OF THAT MOUNTAIN ISN'T GOING TO MAKE IT THIS FAR. TRUST ME, I'M A GEOLOGIST. I KNOW ABOUT THIS STUFF.

FURTHER ALONG THE GREEN RIVER DANNY BALCH AND BRIAN THOMAS HAD SET UP CAMP. THEY WERE SHARING THE CAMP WITH SOME OF BRIAN'S FRIENDS.

YOU'RE QUIET. ARE YOU STILL SORE THAT WE DIDN'T GO TO THE BEACH LIKE YOU WANTED, DANNY?

NO, IT'S NOT THAT. AND I LIKE YOUR FRIENDS, BRIAN.

I KNOW SOME PEOPLE WHO WERE AT THE TOP OF THE MOUNTAIN IN THE WINTER. THEY SAID THE SNOW HAD TURNED INTO SLUSH.

SOMETHING HAD BEEN MELTING IT LONG BEFORE THIS NEW VOLCANO SCARE.

I HAVE A BAD FEELING ABOUT THE MOUNTAIN.

JUST AFTER 8:00 A.M. ON MAY 18, GEOLOGISTS KEITH AND DOROTHY STOFFEL AND PILOT BRUCE JUDSON WERE FLYING TOWARD THE SUMMIT OF MOUNT ST. HELENS.

I'LL TAKE US OVER THE SUMMIT AND THEN COME AROUND AND MAKE A SECOND PASS.

THE MOUNTAIN LOOKS SO PEACEFUL. YOU WOULDN'T THINK IT COULD ERUPT AT ANY MOMENT.

AT COLDWATER 2 OBSERVATION POINT DAVID JOHNSTON BEGAN A DAY OF VOLCANO WATCHING.

AT THE GREEN RIVER DANNY BALCH WAS STILL ASLEEP.

DANNY! ARE YOU GOING TO STAY IN THAT TENT ALL DAY?

NEARBY MIKE AND LU MOORE WERE PLANNING THEIR HIKE FOR THE DAY.

THERE ARE SOME OLD MINES AROUND HERE. WE MIGHT FIND SOME INTERESTING ROCK SAMPLES, WHO KNOWS?

AT SPIRIT LAKE HARRY TRUMAN WAS TAKING CARE OF HIS CATS.

I SUPPOSE YOU CATS WILL BE WANTING YOUR BREAKFAST.

AT 8:32 A.M....

WAIT! SOMETHING'S HAPPENING DOWN THERE.

LOOK AT THAT! THE MOUNTAINSIDE! IT'S JUST SLIDING AWAY!

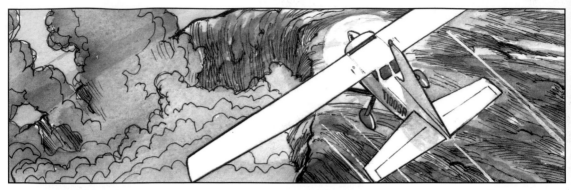

WHILE DOROTHY STOFFEL WATCHED THE LANDSLIDE, KEITH STOFFEL GLANCED OVER HIS SHOULDER.

BRUCE, WE HAVE TO GET OUT OF HERE! **RIGHT NOW!**

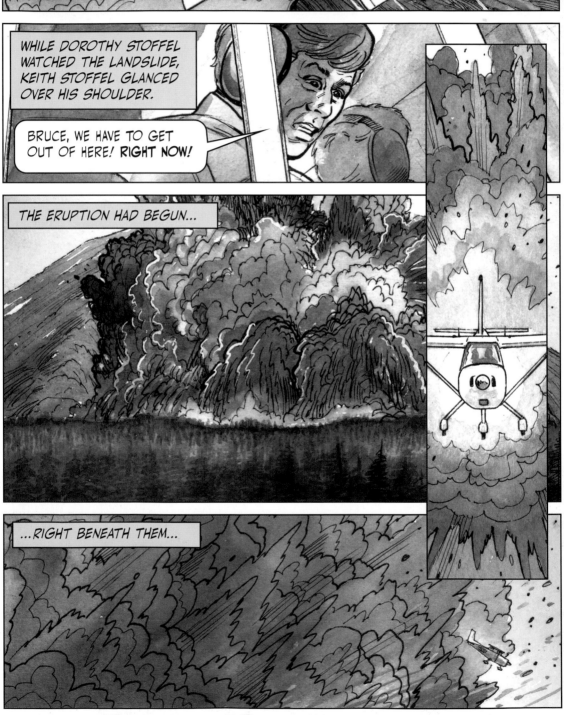

THE ERUPTION HAD BEGUN...

...RIGHT BENEATH THEM...

AT COLDWATER 2...

THE LANDSLIDE SWEPT ON TO HARRY TRUMAN'S LODGE AT SPIRIT LAKE.

VANCOUVER! VANCOUVER! THIS IS IT!

DAVID! DAVID! CAN YOU HEAR ME? COME IN!

AT CASTLE LAKE, WEST OF THE MOUNTAIN, CHARLES MCNERNEY AND JOHN SMART THOUGHT THEY WERE A SAFE DISTANCE AWAY.

RUN!

I THINK IT'S GAINING!

AT THE GREEN RIVER MIKE AND LU MOORE QUICKLY PACKED THEIR CAMPING GEAR AS THE HOT CLOUD APPROACHED.

GET INTO THE HUT. I JUST WANT TO TAKE A FEW PHOTOGRAPHS.

HURRY, MIKE!

THUNDER AND LIGHTNING CRACKLED OUTSIDE THE HUT. INSIDE, THE FINE ASH MADE BREATHING DIFFICULT.

SKREEEAWWW!!

FURTHER ALONG THE GREEN RIVER THE BLAST WAVE HIT DANNY BALCH AND HIS FRIENDS.

SUE RUFF AND BRUCE NELSON WERE THROWN INTO A HOLLOW WHICH PROTECTED THEM.

BRIAN THOMAS WAS CAUGHT IN THE OPEN. AFTER THE BLAST, ICE-COLD MUDDY RAIN FELL.

THEN CAME THE BOILING CLOUD OF HOT ASH.

WHEN IT WAS OVER BRIAN THOMAS WAS BADLY BURNED AND DANNY BALCH HAD BROKEN HIS HIP. SUE RUFF AND BRUCE NELSON WERE UNHURT BUT TERRY CALL AND KAREN VARNER WERE MISSING.

WHEN THE MOUNTAIN EXPLODED SNOW AND ICE MELTED. THE MELTWATER FORMED LAHARS, FAST RIVERS OF MUD AND ASH.

NOTHING COULD STAND IN THEIR WAY.

WHEN THE RIVERS OF MUD STOPPED THEY DRIED AS HARD AS CONCRETE.

CHARLES MCNERNEY AND JOHN SMART HAD FINALLY OUTRAN THE DEADLY CLOUD.

WE MUST HAVE BEEN DOING OVER A HUNDRED MILES AN HOUR BACK THERE.

DANNY BALCH AND BRIAN THOMAS HAD BEEN BADLY INJURED IN THE BLAST. TERRY CALL AND KAREN VARNER HAD BEEN CRUSHED TO DEATH BY FALLING TREES. SUE RUFF AND BRUCE NELSON SET OFF TO GET HELP. ALL FOUR SURVIVORS WERE RESCUED.

THE MOORE FAMILY LEFT THEIR SHELTER AND STARTED TO WALK OUT OF THE FOREST.

I THINK IT MIGHT BE THIS WAY. I CAN'T TELL WHERE THE TRAIL IS UNDER ALL THIS ASH.

EVENTUALLY THE MOORES REACHED THE EDGE OF THE STANDING FOREST. THEY WERE LOST.

THE MOORES WERE NOT FOUND UNTIL THE FOLLOWING DAY. THEY WERE PICKED UP BY A NATIONAL GUARD HELICOPTER.

THAKKA THAKKA THAKKA

FROM THE HELICOPTER THEY SAW THE DEVASTATION THAT THE ERUPTION HAD CAUSED.

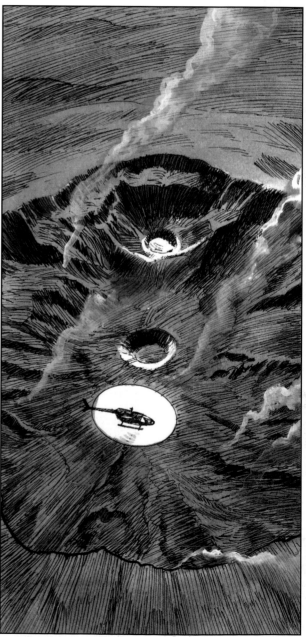

57 PEOPLE DIED THAT DAY, INCLUDING HARRY TRUMAN AND DAVID JOHNSTON. IN 1997 COLDWATER RIDGE WAS RENAMED JOHNSTON RIDGE IN HIS MEMORY. TODAY VISITORS TO THE JOHNSTON RIDGE OBSERVATORY CAN WATCH THE VOLCANO. IN ITS CRATER A 500-FOOT (152-METER) DOME MADE OF LAVA HAS GROWN.

THE END

STUDYING VOLCANOES

Predictions of exactly when a volcano will erupt can be made around 24–48 hours in advance. In most cases this is enough time to evacuate people in the danger area. However, there are places where millions of people live in the shadow of a volcano. Popocatépetl, overlooking Mexico City, has come to life again and Mount Etna threatens people living on the east of Sicily, Italy. These are just two of many places where evacuating all the people in danger may take longer than 48 hours.

Mount Etna is one of the most active volcanoes in the world. The photograph (above) from space shows an eruption in 2002. The most recent was in 2006.

THE SIGNS

Volcanologists are continually studying and measuring volcanoes around the world. Signs they look out for are: seismic activity (earthquakes and tremors), gas emissions (when magma nears the surface, sulfur dioxide gas increases), ground bulges (as magma builds up it can push up the ground), hydrology (rivers flowing from volcanoes can carry signs of increased volcanic activity), satellite information (satellites can sense changes in heat and sulfur dioxide emissions), and local predictions (people living near a volcano may notice repeated signals from previous eruptions.)

In December 2000, scientists warned that Popocatépetl was about to erupt. 26,000 people were evacuated from the area, but just as many refused to leave their farms. The volcano is still active today and scientists are monitoring it very closely.

A volcanologist's job can be dangerous. He or she might be poisoned by toxic sulfur dioxide gas from the crater floor of Mount St. Helens (above) or burned when taking lava, such as from a Hawaiian volcano (inset). Satellites send data about the gas and heat of volcanoes like Sakurajima (below), in Japan.

Volcanic eruptions can devastate the habitat surrounding a volcano. However it doesn't take long for vegetation and wildlife to return. Fireweed (below) began reappearing on the slopes of Mount St. Helens within a few months.

GLOSSARY

blast wave A moving wall of compressed air that travels outward from an explosion.

evacuate To send people away from a threatened area.

geologist Scientist who studies the Earth's crust and layers.

habitat An area of particular animal and plant life.

molten Made liquid by heat.

plinian A type of volcanic eruption with a high column of ash, described by Pliny the Younger, who wrote about the Vesuvius eruption in A.D. 79.

predicting Saying what will happen in the future.

pumice stones Ejected from volcanoes, these stones, once they have cooled, are very light due to the air bubbles inside them.

pyroclastic flow A fast-moving cloud of hot ash and lava fragments that travels down a volcano's slope.

seismic Tremors in the ground.

silica A white or colorless compound found in rock and magma. It is the main ingredient in making glass.

sulfur dioxide A poisonous gas.

tsunami A large, destructive wave created by a large earth movement, either from an undersea earthquake or a volcanic island exploding.

VEI Volcanic Explosivity Index. The index by which a volcano's strength is classified (see below).

volcanologist Scientist who studies volcanoes.

VEI	Description	Plume height (miles)	Plume height (kilometers)	Classification	How often
			VOLCANIC EXPLOSIVITY INDEX (VEI)		
0	non-explosive	< 0.062	< 0.1	Hawaiian	daily
1	gentle	0.062–0.62	0.1–1	Haw/Strombolian	daily
2	explosive	0.62–3	1–5	Strom/Vulcanian	weekly
3	severe	1.9–9.3	3–15	Vulcanian	yearly
4	cataclysmic	6.2–15.5	10–25	Vulc/Plinian	10s of years
5	paroxysmal	>15.5	>25	Plinian	100s of years
6	colossal	>15.5	>25	Plinian/Ultra-Plinian	100s of years
7	super-colossal	>15.5	>25	Ultra-Plinian	1,000s of years
8	mega-colossal	>15.5	>25	Ultra-Plinian	10,000s of years

Examples: **0.** Kilauea, **1.** Stromboli, **2.** Galeras, 1992, **3.** Ruiz, 1985, **4.** Galunggung, 1982, **5.** Mount St. Helens, 1980, **6.** Krakatoa, 1883, **7.** Tambora, 1815, **8.** Yellowstone, 2 million years ago
Key: < less than, > more than

FOR MORE INFORMATION

ORGANIZATIONS

National Oceanic & Atmospheric Administration (NOAA)
http://www.noaa.gov

The Science Factory
2300 Leo Harris Parkway
Eugene,
Oregon 97401
info@sciencefactory.org
www.sciencefactory.org

FOR FURTHER READING

Arvetis, Chris. *What Is a Volcano?* (Just Ask). Checkerboard Pr., 1983.

Dennis, Peter and Nicholas Harris. *Volcano* (Fast Forward Books). Hauppage, NY: Barron's Educational Series, 2001.

Duval, Stu. *Volcano Adventure* (Science Comic Books). Los Angeles, CA: Nature Publishing House, 1998.

Lampton, Christopher. *Volcano* (Disaster!) Minneapolis, MN: Millbrook Press, 1991.

Morris, Neil. *Volcanoes* (The Wonders of Our World). Ontario, Canada: Crabtree Publishing Company, 1995.

Van Rose, Susanna. *Volcano & Earthquake* (Eyewitness Books). London, England: DK, 2000.

Volcano (EXPERIENCE). London, England: DK, 2006.

INDEX

A

ash, 5, 6, 7, 14, 19, 28, 38, 39, 40, 41, 46

B

Balch, Danny, 31, 32, 38, 39, 41
Berouw, 27
blast wave, 38, 46

C

Call, Terry, 39, 41
crater, 27, 43, 45

E

earthquake, 10, 46
evacuate, 44, 46

F

Fontana, 17

G

geologist, 30, 32

H

habitat, 45, 46
Herculaneum, 14, 17
hurricane, 25

J

Johnston, David, 29, 32, 43
Judson, Bruce, 32, 34

K

Krakatoa, 6, 18–27, 46

L

lahars, 6, 40
landslide, 34, 36
lava, 4, 5, 6, 43, 45, 46
Lindeman, Johan, 18
Loudon, 18, 22, 25, 26

M

magma, 4, 5, 6, 19, 20, 29, 44, 46
Mayon, 6
McNerney, Charles, 36, 41
molten, 4, 6, 19, 46
Moore family, 30, 33, 35, 38, 41, 42
Mount Etna, 44
Mount St. Helens, 7, 28–43, 45

N

Nelson, Bruce, 39, 41

P

plinian, 6, 7, 46
Polybius, Julius, 8, 9, 13, 15, 16
Pompeii, 6, 8, 10, 12, 14, 15, 16, 17
Popocatépetl, 44

predicting, 44, 46
pumice stones, 12, 15, 19, 26, 46
pyroclastic flow, 6, 14, 21, 46

R

Ruff, Sue, 39, 41

S

Santorini, 6
seismic, 44, 46
silica, 6, 46
Smart, John, 36, 37, 41
Stoffel, Dorothy, 32, 34
Stoffel, Keith, 32, 34
sulfur dioxide, 44, 45, 46
Swanton, Don, 29

T

Telok Belong, 18, 23, 27
Thomas, Brian, 31, 39, 41
Truman, Harry, 28, 33, 36, 43
tsunami, 6, 7, 18, 22, 46

V

Varner, Karen, 39, 41
VEI, 46
Vesuvius, 8–17, 46
volcanologist, 29, 44, 45

Web Sites

Due to the changing nature of Internet links, the Rosen Publishing Group, Inc., has developed an online list of Web sites related to the subject of this book. This site is updated regularly. Please use this link to access the list:

http://www.rosenlinks.com/gnd/volc